The Night Before Jesus

Text by Robert F. Heise

Illustrations by John Wade

DOGWOOD PRESS   Greensboro

The Night Before Jesus

First Edition
Manufactured in the United States of America.

ISBN 0-9627049-0-3

Dedication

This book is dedicated to my five granddaughters, Carrie, Lindsey and Martha Heise and Laura and Kelly Byrd, whose expressions and reactions to this poem when I read it on Christmas Eve inspired me to publish this book.

My thanks also to John Wade of Graham, N.C. for his illustrations, and to Martin Hester of Tudor Publishers for his encouragement and assistance.

The Night Before Jesus

It was the night before Jesus, when all through the land
Not a creature was stirring, not even a lamb.

The sun had gone down behind the hill
And the night was silent and still.

The shepherd had just laid down to go to sleep
But that was all right, because so had his sheep.

When out of Heaven what did appear?
An angel who said, "Fear not, for I bring you tidings of good cheer.

A child is born in Bethlehem, and it's a boy!"
The shepherd jumped up and shouted with joy.

A star in the East was shining bright;
It guided three wise men through the night.

Through the desert the camels were moving slow
As the star cast a shadow on the sand below.

13

When in the distance the stable did appear,
The wise men were glad they finally were here.

The star stood still and its light, on the child made a halo.
And Mary and Joseph, how their faces did glow.

The wise men brought gifts of gold and frankincense and myrrh
For they knew a Saviour's birth never again would occur.

18

They looked into the manger and saw a baby so tender and mild
And knelt down to worship Jesus, the Holy Child.

He was all wrapped in swaddling clothes, from His head to His feet.
How beautiful He looked for the people to meet!

22

His eyes how they sparkled from the star's bright beam!
The shepherd felt as if he were having a dream.

Could this not be a dream, and come to pass?
No, because this was Christ the Lord, and His glory would last.

He was born to save the people of the earth,
And that is the reason for the Christ child's birth.

The wise men departed, and went west that day,
For God had told them to return another way.

29

And you could hear the angel exclaim as to Heaven she did ascend:
"Glory to God in the highest, and on earth peace and good will toward men."